outpost zero

CREATED BY SEAN KELLEY MCKEEVER & ALEXANDRE TEFENKGI

FOR SKYBOUND ENTERTAINMENT ROBERT KIRKMAN Chairman DAVID ALPERT
CEO SEAN MACKIEWICZ SVP, Editor-in-Chief SHAWN KIRKHAM SVP, Business
Development BRIAN HUNTINGTON VP, Online Content JUNE ALIAN Publicity
Director ANDRES JUAREZ Art Director JON MOISAN Editor ARIELLE BASICH
Associate Editor CARINA TAYLOR Production Artist PAUL SHIN Business Development Coordinator JOHNNY
O'DELL Social Media Manager SALLY JACKA Skybound Retailer Relations DAN PETERSEN Sr. Director of Operations
& Events International Inquiries ag@sequentialrights.com Licensing Inquiries contact@skybound.com
WWW.SKYBOUND.COM

IMAGE COMICS, INC. ROBERT KIRKMAN Chief Operating Officer ERIK LARSEN
Chief Financial Officer TODD MCFARLANE President MARC SILVESTRI
Chief Executive Officer JIM VALENTINO Vice President ERIC STEPHENSON
Publisher / Chief Creative Officer COREY HART Director of Sales JEFF BOISON
Director of Publishing Planning & Book Trade Sales CHRIS ROSS Director of
Digital Sales JEFF STANG Director of Specialty Sales KAT SALAZAR Director
of PR & Marketing DREW GILL Art Director HEATHER DOORNINK Production
Manager NICOLE LAPALME Controller WWW.IMAGECOMICS.COM

THE SMALLEST TOWN IN THE UNIVERSE

SEAN KELLEY McKEEVER
CREATOR/WRITER

ALEXANDRE TEFENKGI
CREATOR/ARTIST

JEAN-FRANCOIS BEAULIEU
COLORIST

ARIANA MAHER
LETTERER

ARIELLE BASICH
ASSOCIATE EDITOR

SEAN MACKIEWICZ
EDITOR

SPECIAL THANKS TO CLIFF CHIANG

OUTPOST ZERO VOLUME 1. FIRST PRINTING. November 2018. Published by Image Comics, Inc. Office of publication: 2701 NW Vaughn St., Ste. 780, Portland, OR 97210. Originally published in single magazine form as OUTPOST ZERO #1-4. OUTPOST ZERO™ (including all prominent characters featured herein), its logo and all character likenesses are trademarks of Skybound, LLC, unless otherwise noted. Image Comics® and its logos are registered trademarks and copyrights of Image Comics, Inc.

volume one

ALL HEALED UP, I SEE.

WHAT DID IT LOOK LIKE? THE CELL.

WE DIDN'T ACTUALLY SEE IT. JUST RADAR.

BUT IT'S AS BIG AS THEY'RE SAYING, WE HAVE TO MAKE SURE WE'RE LOCKED DOWN.

S-STEVEN...

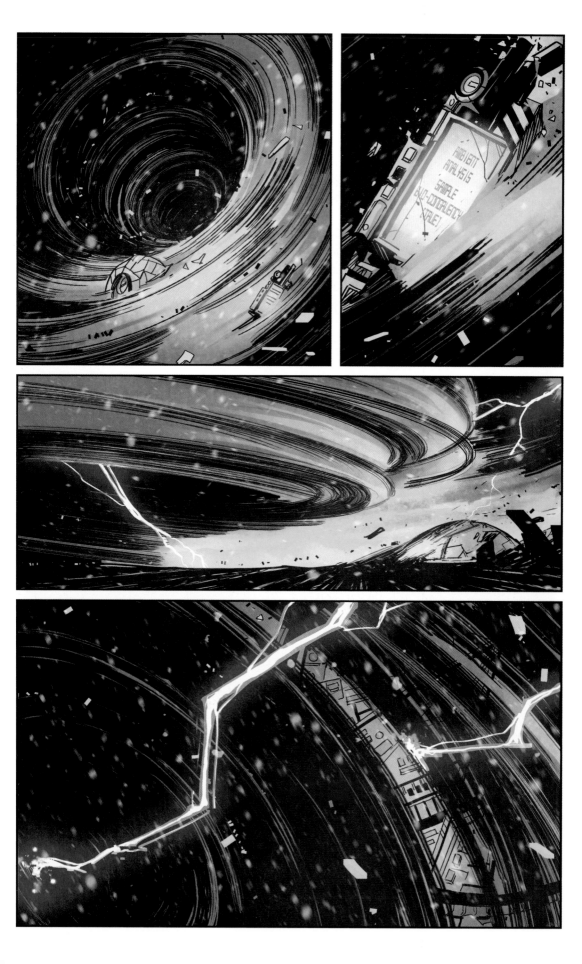

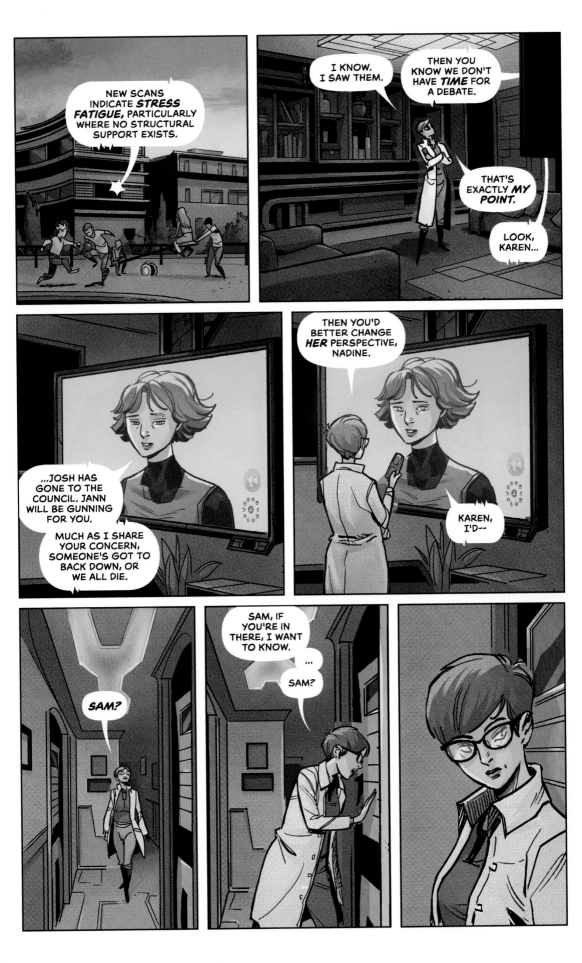

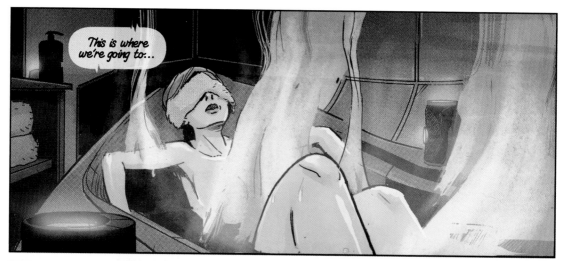

THIS ABOUT, KAREN?

YOUR DAUGHTER...

WHAT ABOUT MY DAUGHTER?

UH. THIS MIGHT SOUND--

BUT, UH...

DO YOU *TRUST* HER?

THE *POINT* OF THAT KIND OF QUESTION HAD BETTER MAKE ITSELF *KNOWN* BEFORE--

IT'S OKAY. I DON'T--

JUST...

YOU GIVE HER SPACE. YOU WANT HER TO LEARN FROM EXPERIENCE, YOU HOPE SHE'LL MAKE THE RIGHT CHOICES...

...BUT THERE'S A *LINE,* RIGHT? THERE'S A POINT WHERE YOU HAVE TO STEP IN, TAKE CONTROL.

to be
continued

i wish i could
be there.
wish i could
see all the
incredible,
alien things.

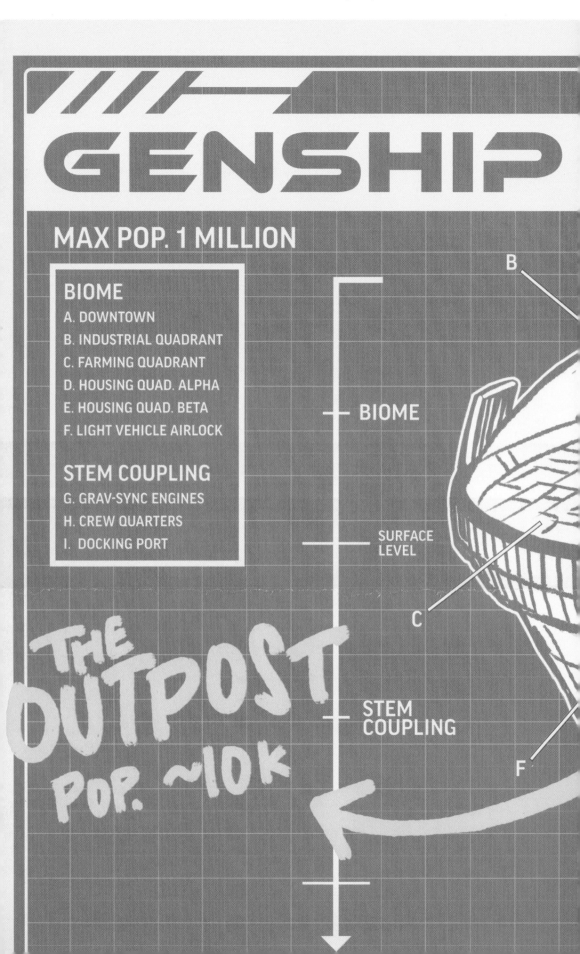

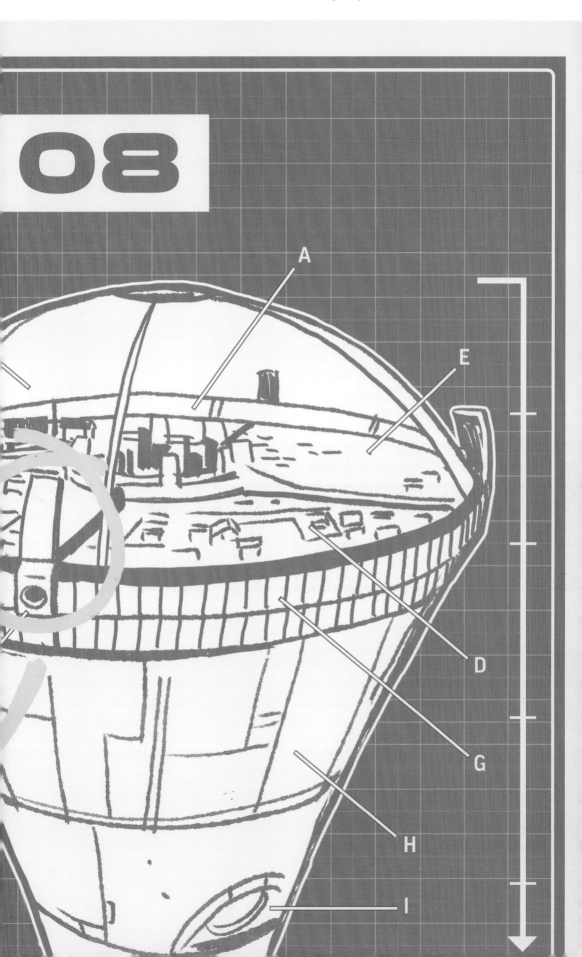

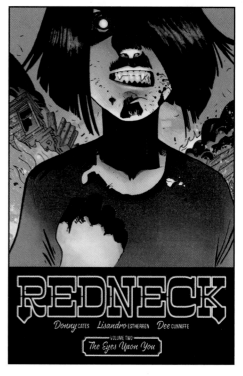